Reinach   6/23/80

Me Too Iguana

DATE DUE

JAN. 24	1981	AUG. 1 8	1988
FEB. 9	1981	AUG. 2 7	1984
FEB. 2 1	1981	DEC. 2 7	1984
MAR. 2 3	1981	FEB. 9	1985
APR. 5	1981	JAN. 1 7	1985
MAY 4	1981	SEP 2 1	1985
JUN. 2 9	1981	NOV 1 8	1986
NOV. 9	1981	OCT. 1 8	1986
DEC. 26	1981	SEP. 1 0	1987
MAY 1 5	1982	JAN. 2 8	1988
JUN. 2 1	1982	NOV. 2 8	1992
JAN. 3	1983	JUN 0 3	1999

OEMCO

THIS

SWEET PICKLES ®

BOOK
BELONGS TO

In the world of *Sweet Pickles,* each animal
gets into a pickle because of an all too human
personality trait.

This book is about Imitating Iguana who
wants to be just like everybody else.

Other Books in the Sweet Pickles Series

STORK SPILLS THE BEANS
ZEBRA ZIPS BY
GOOSE GOOFS OFF
VERY WORRIED WALRUS
FIXED BY CAMEL

Library of Congress Cataloging in Publication Data

Reinach, Jacquelyn.
  Me too, Iguana.

  (Sweet Pickles series)
  SUMMARY : The residents of Sweet Pickles try to help
Iguana who wants to be like everyone else she sees.
  [1. Iguana–Fiction] I. Hefter, Richard, ill.
II. Title. III. Series.
PZ7.R2747Me   [E]   76-43090
ISBN 0-03-018071-6

Printed in the United States of America

Weekly Reader Books' Edition

Weekly Reader Books presents

ME TOO
IGUANA

Written by Jacquelyn Reinach
Illustrated by Richard Hefter
Edited by Ruth Lerner Perle

Holt, Rinehart and Winston · New York

Iguana had a lovely green color...and a long bumpy tail ... and an apartment...and a balcony with a tree growing on it.

But Iguana wasn't satisfied with her lovely green color...or her long bumpy tail...or anything else she had. Whatever anybody else had, she wanted too.

At the supermarket, Iguana saw Elephant, the manager, lifting cans of soup with her trunk.

"A trunk!" cried Iguana. "Me too! Me too! I want a trunk too!"

So Iguana went home and cut a piece of rubber hose. She painted it grey and tied it to her nose.

"Good!" said Iguana. "Now I have a trunk too."

At the barbershop, Iguana saw Lion getting his mane trimmed.

"A mane!" cried Iguana. "Me too! Me too! I want a mane too!"

So Iguana went home and stuck a lot of thick yellow wool all over her head.

"Good!" said Iguana. "Now I have a trunk and a mane too."

At the car wash, Iguana watched Zebra taking a shower.
His black and white stripes gleamed in the sunlight.
"Stripes!" cried Iguana. "Me too! Me too! I want stripes too!"
So Iguana went home to make stripes.

On the way, Iguana saw Goose taking a nap. Her feathers were flapping in the breeze.

"Feathers!" cried Iguana. "Me too! Me too! I want feathers too!"

So Iguana went home to make stripes like Zebra and feathers like Goose.

First she opened two jars of paint. She took a wide brush and painted stripes on her sides. Then she shook the feathers out of an old pillow and glued them on her back.

"Good!" said Iguana. "Now I have a trunk and a mane and stripes and feathers too!"

Everybody wondered what Iguana was doing. Why was she imitating them?

"Ohhh," worried Walrus, "this could get to be a problem."

At the post office, Stork was flying in with the air mail delivery. "Flying!" cried Iguana. "Me too! Me too! I want to fly too!" So she went home to figure out how to make wings.

"Ohhh, this *is* a problem," said Walrus. "Iguana can't fly. She'll hurt herself!"

Everybody agreed. This "me too" business had to stop before it was too late.

But how?

"Why would a nice Iguana with a lovely green color and a long bumpy tail want a trunk and mane and stripes and all the rest?" asked Lion.

"Why?" everybody wondered.

"Because," said Zebra, "she must think that a trunk and a mane and stripes and all the rest are better."

"But how do we stop her?" wondered Elephant.

"That's a good question," said Stork.

Everybody thought and whispered and scratched heads. Finally they had a plan. They wrote a letter.

Stork dropped the letter on Iguana's balcony.

"Everybody come to a costume party at the playground," it said. *"All costumes must be kept secret. NO TALKING ABOUT THEM!"*

Iguana forgot all about wanting to fly. "A costume party!" she cried. "Me too! Me too! Everybody will be there. I'll be there too!"

"But what will I do for a costume?" she cried. "I want to wear what everybody else is wearing too!"

When it was time for the party, Iguana still didn't have a costume. She sneaked into the playground and hid behind a tree.

In the distance, behind the swings, she saw a flash of green. Near the jungle gym, she saw another flash of green. By the fountains, a flash of green. What was going on?

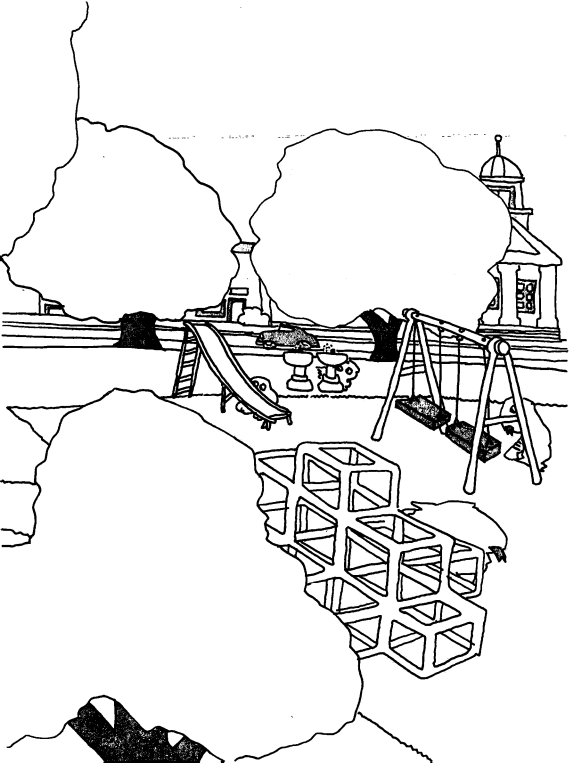

"Oh! Nobody has a trunk!" cried Iguana. Quickly, she took off her trunk.

"Oh! Nobody has a mane!" she cried. She pulled off her mane.

"Oh! Nobody has stripes! Nobody has feathers!"

Iguana wiped off the stripes and pulled off the feathers.
Then she moved closer to get a better look.

Everybody's costume was a lovely green color. Everybody had a long bumpy tail.

EVERYBODY WAS DRESSED AS AN IGUANA!

"Come, join the party!" they called. "You're dressed perfectly!"

"But I'm not wearing a costume," cried Iguana. "This is just plain me."

Then Stork said, "There is a prize for the best Iguana. And the prize goes to…" He turned slowly around. "The prize goes to…IGUANA! You have the loveliest, greenest color," smiled Stork. "You have the longest, bumpiest tail. Congratulations! We all think you're wonderful just the way you are!"

"Yes," said Iguana, very surprised, "I do too!"

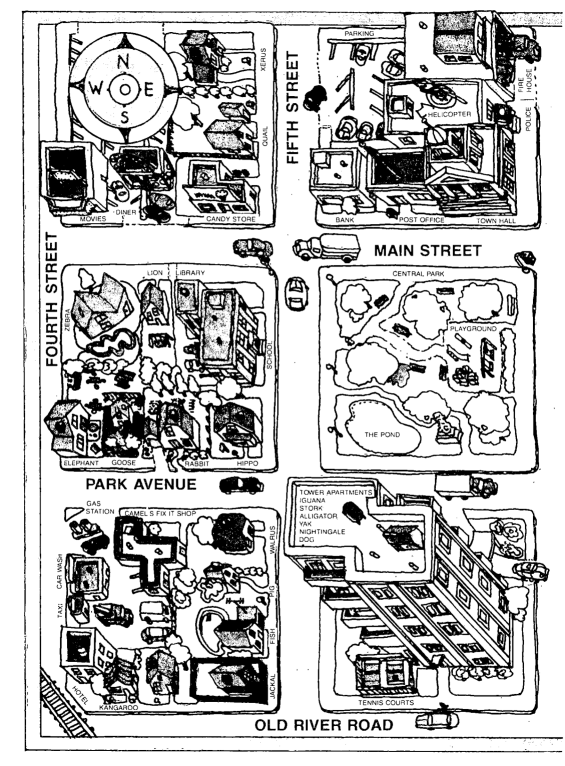